INTROSPECTION

ESHAAN TIWARI

Made with ♥ on the Notion Press Platform
www.notionpress.com

To those who dare to look within,
To the seekers of truth and the dreamers of growth,
May your journey be as enlightening as your destination.

Contents

Acknowledgements

This book would not have been possible without the support, inspiration, and encouragement of many people.

To my family, thank you for always believing in me and providing the space for my creativity to flourish. Your unconditional faith in my abilities has been my greatest source of strength.

To my friends, thank you for listening to my ideas, sharing your thoughts, and encouraging me to take this leap. Your honest feedback and constant motivation pushed me to give my best.

To every teacher, mentor, or guide who has ever nurtured my love for words, thank you for planting the seeds of curiosity and expression in me.

Finally, to you, the reader, thank you for picking up this book and taking the time to explore my journey. Your presence gives meaning to my words; I am deeply grateful for that.

This book reflects everyone who has touched my life, directly or indirectly. Thank you for being a part of my story.

Foreword

In the fast-paced world we live in today, there is a subtle yet ever-present tendency to equate success with the accumulation of accolades and external achievements. Yet, as Introspection: The Journey Within reminds us, true success is far more significant. It is measured not by what we gain outwardly, but by the depth of understanding we cultivate inwardly.

Through the deeply reflective and richly human story of Arvind Rathor, Eshaan Tiwari offers us a mirror—an opportunity to examine our motivations, fears, and aspirations. What makes this work so compelling is its authenticity. Arvind's challenges—his struggle with ego, his sense of isolation, and his ultimate rediscovery of connection and purpose—resonate universally.

To anyone who has ever felt the weight of expectations or the sting of failure, this book offers both solace and inspiration. It is proof to the power of introspection and the strength of the human spirit.

Prologue

Hillspring Academy stood nestled in the calmness of emerald hills, its buildings are a testament to decades of academic excellence. To outsiders, it was a beacon of achievement, a place where dreams were forged and futures were shaped. But for those within its walls, it was also a home—a space where ambition and pressure collided, leaving scars that were often invisible.

Arvind Rathor, a fourteen-year-old prodigy, entered these halls with a singular vision: to excel. What he didn't anticipate was how the pursuit of greatness would lead him to lose sight of himself. This is the story of how he found his way back—not through triumphs, but through introspection, through the quiet moments of self-discovery that turned a star student into a whole person.

Preface

The journey to understanding oneself is neither straightforward nor swift. It is a path marked by missteps, reflection, and gradual growth. Introspection: The Journey Within was born from the recognition that so many of us juggle with the balance between ambition and authenticity. In Arvind Rathor's story, I hope you find glimpses of your struggles, triumphs, and the quiet moments that define true growth.

This book is not just about a young boy in a boarding school; it's about all of us—students of life, learning to navigate the complexities of relationships, goals, and ever-longing self-discovery. I hope that Arvind's journey inspires you to reflect on your own, highlighting both the highs and the lows as integral parts of the whole.

The Beginning

CHAPTER ONE

THE PRODIGY AT HILLSPRING ACADEMY

Arvind Rathor gazed out of the towering windows of the Hillspring Academy's library, where sunlight streaked across rows of bookshelves and illuminated the history of countless scholars who had come before him. At just 14 years old, he had already etched his name among the school's brightest. Teachers often spoke of him with admiration and expectation, holding him as a standard for the rest of the students to aspire to. His academic scores—90% and above in every exam—were the envy of his peers. More than just numbers, Arvind had a natural flair for debating and a mind that dissected arguments with precision.

Last week's interschool debate had been another feather in his cap. Clutching the "Best Speaker Award" in his hand, he walked off the stage to the sound of roaring applause, basking in the attention of students and teachers alike. Yet, for all the acclaim, it wasn't just his oratory or academics that stood out. Arvind was also a poet. His words had a knack for painting vivid pictures of his thoughts, earning him publication in the school's literary magazine.

"What are you scribbling now?" came a familiar voice. Arvind looked up to see Rahul Mehra grinning at him. Tall and athletic, Rahul had an aura of effortless confidence. He excelled in sports and academics, making him a favorite among students and teachers. Yet Rahul's nature was starkly different from Arvind's. While Arvind craved perfection and recognition, Rahul had a way of focusing on himself, pushing for excellence without needing validation from others.

"A poem," Arvind replied, flipping his notebook shut. "Just something about the debate last week."

Rahul smirked. "You and your poems. Let me guess... you wrote about how you crushed the other school's team?"

"Not exactly," Arvind said, rolling his eyes. "It's more about the feeling of being on stage, the adrenaline, the challenge."

"Of course," Rahul teased, ruffling Arvind's hair. "The philosopher strikes again."

Their conversation was interrupted by Kabir Sharma, who approached with his signature calm demeanor. Slightly shorter than the other two but with an air of quiet wisdom, Kabir was the anchor of their trio. He set his books down and surveyed the scene. "What's the topic today?" he asked, his voice steady.

"Arvind's latest masterpiece," Rahul quipped. "But we were just talking about how this genius managed to take all the glory at the debate."

Kabir gave Arvind a small nod of approval. "You deserved it. Though you might want to slow down a bit. You've been running on all cylinders lately."

Arvind waved the comment off. "I'm fine. It's not like I'm struggling."

But even as he said it, he couldn't shake the feeling that Kabir's words carried some truth. With every success came the growing weight of expectations. The conversation shifted as the trio made their way to the dining hall, their laughter echoing through the corridors. For now, Arvind was at the top of his game, unaware of the challenges that lay ahead—challenges that would test not just his abilities, but his character as well.

CHAPTER TWO

The Trio's Balance

The next morning at Hillspring Academy started like any other, with the crisp chill of the hillside air sweeping across the campus grounds. The ringing of the morning bell signaled the students to assemble, but for Arvind, Rahul, and Kabir, mornings often meant huddling under the oak tree in the courtyard before classes began.

Rahul jogged over, fresh from his early morning cricket practice, beads of sweat sliding on his forehead. "Another run scored against the seniors today!" he exclaimed, sitting down and flashing his trademark smile.

"Of course," Arvind said, raising an eyebrow. "You'll be impossible to deal with for the rest of the day."

Kabir chuckled softly, pushing his glasses up. "He's always impossible, but at least he backs it up."

Rahul leaned back against the tree. "Unlike you two philosophers, I engage in activities where you move your body. Imagine that."

"Imagine thinking debates don't count as a sport?" Arvind shot back. "We outwit opponents, dodge rhetorical traps, and land verbal punches. Sounds like a sport to me."

"Keep telling yourself that, buddy," Rahul smirked, pulling out a protein bar from his bag.

The three boys had always complemented each other. Rahul's competitive spirit pushed Arvind to strive harder, while Kabir's calm steadiness often helped to diffuse the intensity. But in recent weeks, Arvind had started noticing an odd pressure. Though they were his best friends, Arvind couldn't help but compare himself to Rahul's natural athleticism and Kabir's quiet intelligence.

At their core, the trio was tight-knit, but cracks had begun to show. Subtle ones. The kind only Arvind was sensitive to—especially as he felt a growing need to prove he wasn't just the best in academics, but the best, period.

The first signs of this tension appeared during their literature class that day. Their teacher, Mrs. Bose, handed back essays and announced the top three students in the class.

"Rahul Mehra," she said, with an approving smile, "an excellent paper as always. First place."

Arvind blinked in surprise. Rahul? Literature wasn't even his strongest subject. But Mrs. Bose wasn't done.

"Kabir Sharma," she continued, "thoughtful analysis and wonderfully articulated. Second place."

The class clapped politely. Arvind's heart raced. Surely, his name would follow.

"Third place... Megha Reddy."

Arvind stared at his desk, the hum of the classroom fading into a dull buzz. Third? He hadn't even placed. Rahul noticed his expression and leaned over with a teasing smile. "Looks like I'm finally catching up."

"Catching up?" Arvind muttered, his voice sharper than intended. "I didn't know this was a competition."

Rahul raised his hands defensively. "Easy there, champ. Just joking."

Kabir frowned slightly, catching the tension. "Arvind, everyone has an off day. Don't sweat it."

But Arvind wasn't ready to let it go. For the rest of the day, he threw himself into his work, scribbling furiously in his notebook during breaks, crafting what he hoped would be a flawless poem for the school's literary magazine. Yet, the thought lingered: if Rahul was excelling in academics and sports, and Kabir was as composed and respected as ever, where did that leave him?

The tension came to a head during the evening debate practice. The team was preparing for an inter-house competition, and Arvind had volunteered to lead the session. It wasn't long before Rahul, who had joined mostly for fun, started throwing out bold, unconventional arguments.

"Rahul," Arvind said, his tone clipped, "that's not going to work in a formal debate. Stick to the structure."

"Why not? It's engaging," Rahul replied. "Isn't the goal to win the audience over?"

"Yes, but not at the expense of strategy," Arvind countered, his frustration spilling out. "Not everything's a cricket match where you can just wing it."

The room fell silent. Rahul's easygoing demeanor shifted, his expression hardening. "And not everything's about playing it safe, Arvind. Maybe you should try loosening up once in a while."

Kabir intervened, his calm voice cutting through the tension. "Alright, let's take a break. This isn't helping anyone."

As the group dispersed, Kabir pulled Arvind aside. "What's going on with you?" he asked, his tone gentle but firm.

"Nothing," Arvind snapped, then immediately softened. "It's just... everything feels like it's slipping. I have to stay ahead, Kabir."

"Stay ahead of who?" Kabir asked, his gaze steady. "Rahul? Me? Or are you just competing with yourself?"

Arvind didn't answer. He didn't know how to. Instead, he muttered something about needing to prepare for exams and walked away, leaving Kabir watching him with quiet concern.

That night, Arvind sat by the window of his dorm room, the cool breeze brushing against his face. In the distance, he could hear Rahul's laughter echoing.

CHAPTER THREE

QUESTION YOURSELF

Arvind's accomplishments at Hillspring Academy seemed never-ending. Another week brought yet another achievement—a top grade in his mathematics exam and his poem, "Reflections of the Sky", being prominently displayed on the school's bulletin board. Students passing by paused to admire his work, while teachers nodded approvingly.

"You're making us all look bad, Arvind," a classmate giggled one afternoon, but there was a bite beneath the humor.

Arvind smiled but shrugged it off. "I'm just doing my best." His modest response felt automatic now, an obligation more than the truth. Deep down, he felt a spark of pride every time someone acknowledged his success.

As accolades piled up, so did his need to keep proving himself. The praise from his parents conveyed through warm letters, fueled his drive. You make us so proud, Arvind, his mother had written. You're a star, and we're sure you'll only keep rising.

But with the rising pressure, Arvind found himself growing restless, even impatient. Rahul's easy charm and ability to excel without apparent effort started irritating him. Kabir's calmness, once a source of inspiration, now felt like a reminder of Arvind's own inner chaos.

"Do you ever take a break?" Rahul asked one afternoon, finding Arvind pouring over debate notes.

"I'll rest when I win the next competition," Arvind replied without looking up.

"Winning isn't everything, you know," Rahul said, his tone light but meaningful.

Arvind laughed, dismissing him. "That's easy to say when you're good at everything."

Rahul raised an eyebrow. "Not everything, Arvind. I just focus on what matters. Maybe you should try that."

The comment stung more than Arvind cared to admit. "Not everyone has the luxury of nailing it, Rahul. Some of us have to work hard."

Rahul let out a short laugh, standing up. "Whatever you say, champ. Just don't burn out."

By the following week, the trio was preparing for an inter-house event—a creative collaboration of debates and performances. Arvind, eager to shine, took charge of their team's efforts.

"We'll lead with the debate, then transition into the spoken word piece," Arvind announced during their planning session.

"I was thinking the reverse," Rahul suggested. "Spoken word first to grab attention, then debate to end strong."

Arvind frowned. "No, it'll break the flow. Trust me on this one."

Kabir, seated quietly, spoke up after a notable time. "I think Rahul's idea has merit. Maybe we should—"

"No, Kabir," Arvind interrupted sharply. "This isn't the time for experimenting. We need to stick with a solid strategy."

The tension was visible, but Kabir gave a small nod, his calm exterior was intact. Rahul, however, crossed his arms, his irritation was evident.

"Fine," Rahul said, his voice clipped. "Your call." he sat down next to Kabir and mumbled something near his ear.

The inter-house event proved to be a bittersweet victory. Arvind delivered an outstanding performance during the debate, earning cheers from the audience and a nod of approval from the judges. Yet, when it came to the spoken word segment, the team's rushed execution showed cracks.

Afterward, Rahul approached Arvind. "Maybe if we'd started with the spoken word, the transition wouldn't have been so clunky and confusing."

"Maybe if you'd put more effort into it, it wouldn't have been 'clunky and confusing' at all," Arvind shot back.

Rahul's eyes narrowed. "You know what, Arvind? You've got a real knack for putting yourself above everyone else. You want all the glory, and when something doesn't work, it's everyone else's fault."

"That's not true!" Arvind shouted, but his voice faltered.

"It is," Rahul said, stepping closer. "And if you keep going like this, you'll end up alone. Think about that."

Rahul's words echoed long after he walked away. Kabir, who had observed the argument from a distance, approached Arvind later.

"Rahul's harsh sometimes, but he's not wrong," Kabir said gently.

Arvind sighed. "Not you too, Kabir. Can't I just have one person who doesn't think I'm the problem?"

Kabir's expression softened. "You're not the problem, Arvind. But maybe your attitude is. You've achieved so much—maybe it's time to start asking why you're doing all this."

Arvind didn't answer. Instead, he retreated to his dorm room, the weight of their words pressing down on him. For the first time, he questioned whether his relentless drive was helping him rise—or slowly pulling him under.

The Fall

THE BREAKING POINT

The final bell rang, releasing Hillspring Academy into the crisp afternoon air. Most students rushed toward the dormitories, eager for a break from classes, but Arvind found himself in the library, pacing between rows of books. His thoughts churned as he glanced at the paper in his hand: a group project outline for their upcoming interschool presentation competition. As the team leader, Arvind had already spent the better part of the week drafting plans, assigning roles, and preparing talking points.

"This needs to be perfect," he muttered to himself, frowning as he crossed out another line on the page.

When Rahul and Kabir finally joined him at the library table, Arvind barely looked up. Rahul plopped down, flipping a cricket ball in his hand, while Kabir placed his books neatly in a corner and slid into his chair.

"We need to rehearse," Arvind announced without a preamble. "The presentation needs a strong opener, and Rahul, your part is lacking clarity."

Rahul stopped mid-flip. "My part?"

"Yes," Arvind replied spontaneously. "Your argument on the historical significance—it's too vague. You need to focus on tying it back to the main theme."

Rahul set the ball down with a thud. "I thought the point was to give variety, not just reiterate your ideas."

Arvind's eyes narrowed. "It's not about my ideas; it's about the team's success. And as the leader, it's my job to ensure we're cohesive."

Kabir cleared his throat, attempting to mediate. "Arvind, Rahul's point does add depth. Maybe we can find a middle ground?"

But Arvind wasn't having it. "Middle ground doesn't win competitions!"

The tension in the room thickened. Rahul leaned forward, his voice low but firm. "You're not listening to anyone anymore, Arvind. Everything has to be your way."

"Because my way works!" Arvind snapped, slamming his notebook shut. "Unlike your half-baked ideas."

Rahul's chair scraped loudly against the floor as he stood. "You know what? Fine. Do it your way. Let's see how far that gets you."

Kabir's calm voice cut through the rising argument. "Guys, this isn't helping."

But neither Arvind nor Rahul was in the mood to listen. Rahul stormed off, leaving a heavy silence in his walk. Kabir stayed behind, his steady gaze fixed on Arvind.

"What?" Arvind asked defensively.

Kabir sighed. "You're pushing too hard. If you keep treating everyone like pawns in your plan, you're going to end up alone."

Arvind scoffed. "You sound just like Rahul."

Kabir didn't respond immediately. Instead, he stood, gathering his books. "Maybe you should think about why."

The days leading up to the competition were marked by an uneasy quiet. Rahul avoided Arvind entirely, and even Kabir seemed distant. Despite the growing friction, Arvind threw himself into perfecting their presentation, convinced that winning would justify his actions.

The competition day arrived, bringing with it a flurry of activity. Hillspring Academy's team filed into the auditorium, their crisp uniforms a stark contrast to the rising storm beneath the surface. Arvind led the way, his confidence unshaken.

The presentation began smoothly. Kabir's section was measured and insightful, earning polite applause. But when it was Rahul's turn, the cracks began to show. His delivery lacked its usual energy, and at one point, he stumbled over a key point. The audience murmured, and Arvind's frustration exploded. When his turn came, he launched into his argument with practiced precision, his words cutting through the room like a blade.

The applause at the end was polite but subdued. As the team exited the stage, Arvind turned to Rahul. "What was that?"

Rahul's eyes flashed with anger. "That was me trying, despite being treated like an afterthought."

Before Arvind could respond, Kabir stepped between them. "Enough. Both of you."

The results were announced later that afternoon. Hillspring Academy placed second, a respectable finish, but far from the victory Arvind had envisioned. As the team moved out of the auditorium, Rahul spoke quietly to Kabir. "I'm done."

Kabir nodded solemnly, casting a glance at Arvind. "You need to fix this," he said before following Rahul.

Arvind stood alone in the hallway, the weight of their words finally settling on his shoulders. For the first time, he wondered if winning was worth the cost of losing his friends.

The days following the competition were eerily quiet. The usual chirpy talks between Arvind, Rahul, and Kabir were conspicuously absent. Rahul, typically a magnetic presence in their group, had begun spending more time with his cricket teammates. Kabir, while still polite, seemed preoccupied and distant. The trio's once-tight bond felt fractured, and Arvind couldn't shake the sense that it was his fault.

For the first time, Hillspring Academy's vibrant campus felt lonely. Arvind noticed how the laughter of other groups echoed through the corridors, a sound that seemed foreign to him now. Sitting alone at lunch, he tried to focus on his notebook, scribbling fragments of poetry that mirrored his growing unease.

What price for glory, when silence fills the air?
Is a crown of laurels worth a throne that's bare?

He sighed, closing the notebook. The words felt hollow, much like the victories that once filled him with pride.

During debate practices later that week, the rift became more apparent. The team was preparing for another interschool event, and without Rahul's energy or Kabir's steadying presence, the sessions felt mechanical. Arvind tried to push through, offering feedback and refining arguments, but his tone lacked warmth. His teammates followed his instructions, but their enthusiasm was fading.

"Good job," Arvind said at the end of a session, though the words felt forced. As the team dispersed, one of the junior members hesitated before approaching him. "Arvind bhaiya, can I say something?"

He nodded, though his patience was thin. "What is it?"

"I think... maybe you should let people speak more? Sometimes it feels like you don't trust us to do our parts."

Arvind stared at the younger student, taken aback. "That's not true. I just want to make sure we're prepared."

The junior member nodded quickly, retreating. "Of course. Sorry."

But the words lingered, adding to the growing chorus of doubts in Arvind's mind.

That evening, Kabir found Arvind in the library, buried in books. "Still at it?" he asked, sliding into the chair across from him.

Arvind looked up, surprised. "What are you doing here?"

"Checking on a friend," Kabir replied simply. "Or trying to, anyway."

Arvind responded to the implication. "I'm fine. Just busy."

Kabir studied him for a moment before speaking. "You're not fine, Arvind. You're pushing everyone away, and you don't even see it."

Arvind's jaw tightened. "If people can't handle me trying to succeed, that's their problem, not mine."

Kabir's expression softened, but his words were firm. "Is it a success if you're the only one clapping? Think about that."

Without waiting for a response, Kabir stood and walked away, leaving Arvind alone with his thoughts. For the first time, the quietness of the library felt oppressive rather than comforting. As he sat there, staring at the empty chair across from him, he couldn't help but wonder if Kabir was right.

Was the applause worth the silence that followed?

The weeks after the competition were a whirlwind of activities, yet for Arvind, the isolation deepened. Hillspring Academy's midterm exams loomed on the horizon, a crucial period where students huddled together in study groups, exchanging notes and leaning on one another for support. But Arvind found himself excluded from the usual camaraderie.

In the past, Rahul and Kabir had been his go-to study partners. Now, Rahul studied with his cricket team members, who welcomed him with open arms. Kabir, ever calm and focused, spent his time in the library with a quiet group of peers who shared his steady approach to preparation. Arvind, meanwhile, poured over his books alone, determined to outperform everyone.

"They'll see," he muttered one evening, flipping through a math textbook. "They'll realize I don't need anyone."

But as the days wore on, the solitude began to weigh on him. He noticed how the study sessions he overheard were filled with laughter and shared moments of discovery. His efforts felt mechanical, they were absent from the joy he once found in learning.

The first cracks in his overconfidence appeared during a physics test. Arvind, who had always prided himself on his meticulous preparation, found himself stumbling over a particularly tricky question. The realization hit him like a bullet: he had overlooked a key concept, one that Rahul had mentioned weeks ago but that Arvind had dismissed as irrelevant.

When the results were announced, Arvind's score, though still high, was not the top of the class. Rahul had surpassed him, as had another student, Megha Reddy. The murmurs among his classmates were subtle but unmistakable.

"Guess even Arvind has his limits," someone whispered.

He clenched his fists, his jaw tightening. But the disappointment wasn't just about the score—it was the growing realization that his isolation was costing him more than he cared to admit.

One evening, Arvind sat in the hostel's common room, his notebook open but untouched. Across the room, Rahul and Kabir were playing chess, their quiet giggles were filling the space. Arvind watched them from a distance, his thoughts a whirlwind of frustration and longing.

Unable to bear it any longer, he approached them. "Mind if I join?"

Rahul glanced up, his expression unreadable. "It's a two-player game."

Kabir, sensing the tension, offered a small smile. "You can take my place next round."

But the moment felt forced, and Arvind knew it. "Never mind," he muttered, retreating to his corner. The rift between them felt wider than ever.

The turning point came during a poetry submission for the school's literary magazine. Arvind, eager to reclaim a sense of validation, poured his energy into crafting a piece he believed would outshine all others. But when the selections were announced, his poem was absent. Instead, a younger student's work had been chosen for its "raw emotion and authenticity."

Arvind's chest tightened as he read the magazine, the words of the selected poems striking a chord he hadn't expected. They were simple yet heartfelt, starkly contrasting the polished but hollow verses he had submitted.

For the first time, Arvind questioned whether his drive for perfection had stripped away the very essence of his passion. Was he writing to express himself, or merely to maintain his image?

CHAPTER FIVE

FRIEND OR FOE?

Arvind watched the cricket field from a distance, his hands stuffed into his blazer pockets as the cheers of students echoed across the campus. Rahul was at the center of the game, his bat poised with the confidence that came so naturally to him. With a decisive crack, the ball sailed through the air, prompting a chorus of applause and chants of his name.

"Rahul! Rahul!"

Arvind turned away, the sound clashing against his thoughts. He had once been part of that crowd, cheering for his best friend. Now, he felt like an outsider looking in.

Their next confrontation happened the following week during a house meeting. The discussion was about team responsibilities for an upcoming cultural fest, and as usual, Arvind had volunteered to lead. Rahul, however, suggested an alternative candidate—a junior student with a strong track record in organizing events.

"I think Aarav would be a great choice," Rahul said, leaning back in his chair. "He's creative and works well with the team."

Arvind stiffened. "Aarav? He's capable, but he doesn't have the experience to handle something on this scale."

"He has the right attitude," Rahul countered. "That's more important than experience."

"And what's that supposed to mean?" Arvind's voice was sharper than he intended.

Rahul met his gaze evenly. "It means people want to work with someone who listens, Arvind."

The room fell silent, and the tension grew. Kabir, sitting between them, shifted uncomfortably but said nothing. Arvind felt his cheeks flush as he realized how many eyes were on him.

"Fine," he said curtly. "Let Aarav handle it. Let's see how far that gets us."

Rahul shook his head, a faint smirk on his lips. "It's not about how far it gets 'us,' Arvind. It's about giving others a chance."

Arvind looked around and saw that one thing he never wished to. He saw agreement in everyone's eyes for Rahul as they got up and left the room in silence.

CHAPTER SIX

Kabir's Silent Departure

The silence between Arvind and Kabir had stretched for weeks. It wasn't the fiery, loud rupture that had defined his fallout with Rahul; it was quieter, softer, but no less devastating. Kabir, the calm presence who had always grounded their trio, now felt like a stranger. They still exchanged polite nods in the corridors and still shared a classroom, but the conversations that once flowed effortlessly had dried up into mere courtesies.

It was a Wednesday evening when Arvind finally noticed just how far Kabir had pulled away. The library—a place where they had spent countless evenings revising notes and discussing poetry—was now Kabir's place to study, but without him. Arvind stood at the library entrance, his bag slung over one shoulder, watching Kabir sit with a group of juniors Arvind had always dismissed as unimportant.

Kabir's head was bent low, patiently explaining a math equation to a boy who looked entirely lost. Occasionally, Kabir would chuckle, offering an encouraging pat on the boy's shoulder. There was something so effortless about it—something Arvind remembered from their study sessions, a time when Kabir would patiently clarify concepts while Arvind pushed ahead, determined to be the best.

But now, Arvind wasn't part of this picture. It stung Arvind deep inside.

Steeling himself, Arvind approached the table. The younger students immediately stiffened, their gazes darting between Arvind and Kabir. Arvind ignored them, pulling up a chair across from Kabir.

"Busy?" Arvind asked, forcing a smile.

Kabir looked up, surprised but composed. "Kind of." He gestured to the half-completed worksheets scattered across the table. "They needed help with algebra."

Arvind glanced at the papers, unimpressed. "Juniors can manage on their own. You don't need to waste your time."

Kabir's expression didn't change. "It's not a waste if they learn something."

Arvind frowned. "What about us? We used to study together—prep for finals, practice debates..."

"You never asked," Kabir said simply. He leaned back in his chair, studying Arvind carefully. "You've been too busy proving yourself."

Arvind opened his mouth to respond, but Kabir wasn't done.

"Look, Arvind," Kabir said softly. "You've changed. And maybe you don't see it, but you're not the same person who used to sit with us after lights-out, scribbling poetry in the margins of your notebook. You're not the same person who laughed at Rahul's terrible jokes, or who listened when people needed to vent. You... you stopped being present."

"That's not true," Arvind protested. "I'm still here. I just have goals—things I need to achieve. Can't you understand that?"

Kabir smiled faintly, but there was sadness behind it. "You think you're achieving everything alone, but you're losing what matters. First Rahul... and now, well..."

Arvind's chest tightened. "And now what?"

Kabir shook his head. "You're smart enough to figure it out."

The conversation ended there. Kabir turned his attention back to the juniors, who hesitantly resumed their work. Arvind sat frozen for a moment before standing abruptly, his chair went scraping against the floor. He left without another word.

The following days were worse. Arvind noticed Kabir spending more time with others—students Arvind had always thought beneath their notice. Kabir was tutoring, mentoring, and laughing with people Arvind had never considered important. It made Arvind furious, though he couldn't understand why.

One afternoon, as Arvind sat alone on a bench by the cricket field, he spotted Kabir talking to Rahul. The two of them looked completely at ease, exchanging smiles and shaking hands before parting ways. Arvind felt his stomach sink.

The realization hit him with the force of a falling brick: Kabir hadn't chosen sides. Kabir hadn't abandoned Rahul or taken some moral stand against Arvind. Kabir had simply... left. Quietly. And in doing so, he had made it clear that he no longer had space for the version of Arvind that now existed.

That evening, Arvind sat on his bed, staring at the pages of his notebook. His once-flowing poetry had dried up into short, disjointed lines.

Between echoes and silence, the answers hide,
But voices once loud now step aside.

He snapped the notebook shut, frustration boiling inside him. Kabir's words replayed in his mind on a loop.

"You've changed."

"You're not present anymore."

Arvind wanted to deny it, but deep down, he couldn't. Rahul's anger and Kabir's quiet departure weren't accidents. They were consequences—consequences of choices Arvind had made, even if he hadn't seen them for what they were at the time.

For the first time in weeks, Arvind didn't open his textbooks. He didn't plan his next 'big accomplishment'. He didn't write or practice. Instead, he sat alone in the dark dormitory, listening to the distant laughter of other students, and let the silence settle over him like a heavy blanket.

The turning point came on a Friday afternoon. Arvind found Kabir sitting beneath an old peepal tree near the edge of campus, a notebook open on his lap. It was a spot they sat frequent together—a place where Arvind had once poured his heart into poems and dreams.

Arvind hesitated before approaching. Kabir looked up as he drew near, his face unreadable.

"Can I sit?" Arvind asked quietly.

Kabir nodded, returning his gaze to the notebook. For a few moments, neither of them spoke. Arvind watched the wind rustle the leaves above them, the scorching sunlight dancing on the ground. Finally, he broke the silence.

"Do you think I'm a bad person?"

Kabir didn't look up. "No. But I think you stopped listening to yourself."

Arvind frowned. "What do you mean?"

Kabir sighed, closing his notebook and meeting Arvind's eyes. "You're so busy proving yourself to everyone that you forgot what you care about. Success, awards, praise—you chased all of it because you thought it would make you happy. But it didn't, did it?"

Arvind opened his mouth, but no words came.

Kabir continued. "You used to love what you did, Arvind. You wrote because you loved it. You debated because you enjoyed the challenge. You studied because you wanted to learn. But somewhere along the way, it stopped being about you. It became about being better than everyone else."

The words hit Arvind like a punch to the gut. He looked away, staring at his hands.

"Can I fix it?" Arvind whispered.

Kabir offered a small smile. "That's up to you."

That night, Arvind sat by his desk, staring at a blank sheet of paper. Slowly, he picked up his pen and began to write—not for praise, not for validation, but for himself. The words came slowly at first, shaky and uncertain, but soon they began to flow.

To lose what matters is not defeat,
But lessons bloom where egos retreat.

For the first time in months, Arvind felt lighter. He kept away the paper and the pen. He walked up to his dormitory. The lights were off, and everyone was buried under their blankets. Arvind sat on his bed, snatched out his socks, and lied on the bed. For the first time he introspected, he thought was he going wrong?

Introspection

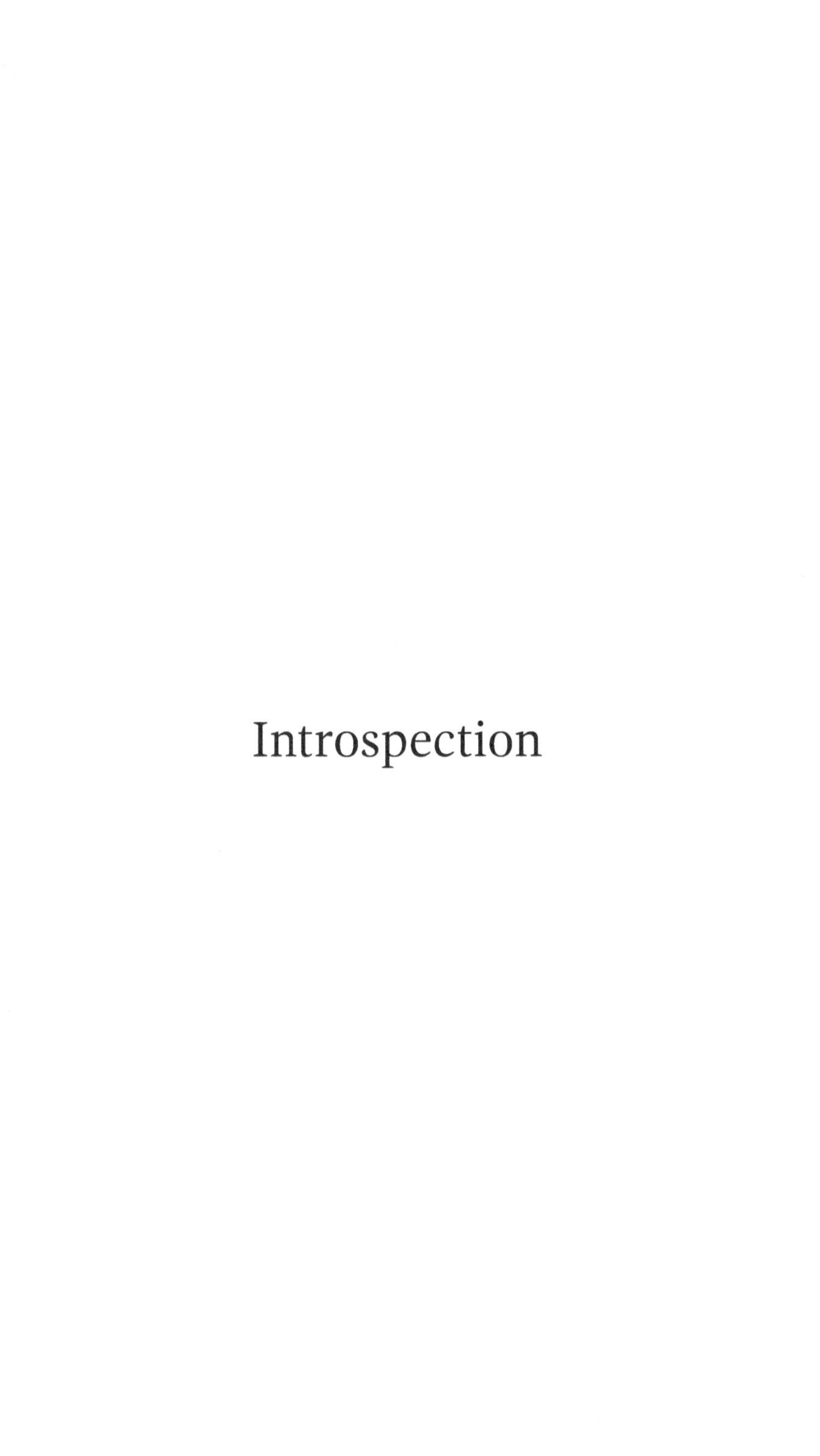

CHAPTER SEVEN

THE ROAD TO REALIZATION

The emptiness of Hillspring Academy's vibrant campus seemed sharper to Arvind now. For weeks, he had brushed past moments of discomfort, dismissing Rahul's anger and Kabir's withdrawal as misunderstandings or petty grievances. But the truth was no longer avoidable. Their words, their silences, had carved deep cracks in his self-assurance. Those cracks threatened to collapse everything he thought he knew about himself.

One Saturday morning, Arvind woke up with an unusual heaviness in his chest. The dormitory was unusually quiet; most of his peers had left for sports practice or weekend study groups. Arvind, however, stayed curled up in bed, his thoughts refusing to let him rest. The memories of Kabir's quiet, measured words under the peepal tree played repeatedly in his mind.

"You're so busy proving yourself to everyone that you forgot what you care about."

He sighed, staring at the ceiling. For the first time in months, he didn't feel the urge to jump into his daily routine. There was no compulsion to perfect his debate arguments or review his notes. Instead, he reached for the notebook on his desk—the one where he had once scribbled poems and stories in the margins of his study materials. Its pages were blank now, absent of the creativity that used to pour out of him effortlessly.

Arvind flipped through the notebook, pausing at an unfinished poem he had written months ago. The lines were abrupt as if they had been abandoned mid-thought:

I chase the sun but lose its glow,
Its warmth is replaced by shadows I know.

His lips tightened. When had I stopped writing? When had I stopped caring about the things that mattered?

By mid-afternoon, Arvind found himself wandering through the campus. The usual spots—the library, the debate hall, even the cricket field—felt foreign to him. He finally stopped at the auditorium, drawn by the faint sound of music. Pushing the heavy doors open, he found a small group of juniors rehearsing a play for the upcoming cultural fest. They were laughing, improvising, and scribbling notes on the back of their scripts. Their energy was infectious, a sharp contrast to the stillness that had taken root in Arvind's life.

One of the students noticed him standing in the doorway. "Arvind, sir!" she called her voice a mix of excitement and nervousness. "Do you want to watch? We're just running through some scenes."

Arvind hesitated before stepping inside. He nodded, taking a seat in the back row. For the next hour, he watched as the students stumbled through their lines, broke into laughter, and cheered each other on. There was a raw, unpolished joy in their efforts that struck a chord deep within him.

When the rehearsal ended, the students gathered their things, still buzzing with excitement. As they left, one of them approached Arvind shyly. "We'd love your feedback, sir. You're so good at public speaking... any tips?"

Arvind blinked, taken aback. *Do they still look up to me? After everything?* He nodded slowly. "Your energy is great. Just remember, the audience connects most with sincerity. Don't worry about being perfect—focus on feeling the moment."

The student beamed, thanking him before hurrying off to join the others. Arvind sat there for a while longer, his words echoing in his mind. *Focus on feeling the moment.*

That evening, Arvind sat by the fountain near the dormitories, a place he had avoided ever since his fallout with Rahul. The soft trickle of water and the golden glow of the setting sun created a serene atmosphere, but Arvind's thoughts were anything but peaceful.

Have I been running from myself? The question darted at him. He thought back to Rahul's parting words, to Kabir's steady gaze, and to the laughter of the juniors in the auditorium. Slowly, a realization began to take shape—a painful but necessary truth.

He had spent so long chasing achievements and external validation that he had lost sight of why he had started in the first place. Writing, debating, studying—they had once been sources of joy and self-expression. But somewhere along the way, they had become tools for proving his worth to others. And in the process, he had alienated the people who mattered most.

The next day, Arvind made his way to the library. He wasn't there to study or to craft the perfect argument for an upcoming debate. Instead, he was looking for Kabir.

He found him sitting in his usual spot by the window, a pile of books spread out before him. Kabir looked up as Arvind approached, his expressions were calm but guarded.

"Hey," Arvind said softly, sliding into the chair across from him. "Can we talk?"

Kabir closed his book, studying Arvind carefully. "Sure."

Arvind hesitated, searching for the right words. "I've been thinking about what you said. About how I... lost sight of what mattered."

Kabir didn't respond immediately, giving Arvind the space to continue.

"I think you're right," Arvind admitted, his voice was barely above a whisper. "I've been so focused on being the best that I forgot why I started in the first place. I... I let my ego take over. And I'm sorry. For everything."

Kabir's gaze softened, but he didn't let Arvind off the hook so easily. "Why are you saying this now?"

Arvind took a deep breath. "Because I don't want to lose you. Or Rahul. Or anyone else. I want to be better—not just for myself, but for the people I care about."

For a long moment, Kabir said nothing. Then, he nodded slowly. "It's not about what you say, Arvind. It's about what you do. If you're serious about this, show it."

Arvind nodded, determination flickering in his eyes. "I will. I promise."

CHAPTER EIGHT

REBUILDING THE BONDS

The air in Hillspring Academy felt lighter to Arvind as he walked through the familiar corridors the next morning. He wasn't sure if the academy itself had changed or if it was him, but for the first time in months, he felt ready to rebuild what he had broken. His heart still carried the weight of past mistakes, but now it was supported by a quiet determination: he would mend his friendships, even if it took time.

Arvind's first step to rebuilding his bonds was his long-lost best friend, Rahul Mehra. Rahul often seemed far apart from Arvind now, which he never used to do. Arvind gathered his guts and decided to move a step ahead of his selfishness and longing ego.

Finding Rahul wasn't difficult. The cricket field had become his sanctuary, a place where he could lose himself in the rhythm of a bat and ball. Arvind stood at the edge of the field, watching as Rahul struck shot after shot with precision, the sound of the bat meeting the ball echoing through the air.

When the practice session ended, Rahul picked up his water bottle and glanced in Arvind's direction. His expression didn't change, but there was no animosity in his eyes either.

"Rahul," Arvind called out, walking toward him. "Can we talk?"

Rahul hesitated before shrugging. "Sure. What is it?"

"I—" Arvind paused, the words he had rehearsed in his mind suddenly feeling inadequate. "I owe you an apology."

Rahul raised an eyebrow but said nothing, letting Arvind continue.

"I've been... awful," Arvind admitted, his voice steady despite the knot in his stomach. "To you, to Kabir, to everyone. I let my ego take over, and I pushed you away. I thought I was doing what I had to do to succeed, but I see now that I was wrong."

Rahul crossed his arms, his face was unreadable. "And what gave birth to this sudden realization?"

"Losing you and Kabir," Arvind said honestly. "I thought I could handle everything on my own, but I can't. I don't want to. I miss having you both in my life."

Rahul studied him for a long moment before sighing. "You know, Arvind, I never stopped rooting for you. Even when you were being insufferable." He smirked slightly. "But words only go so far. Show me you've changed, and maybe we'll get back to where we were."

Arvind nodded, relief washing over him. "I will. Thank you, Rahul."

Rahul gave him a pat on the shoulder before heading off to join his teammates. It wasn't a complete rebound, but it was a start.

Next, Arvind turned his attention to the debate team.

Over the past months, he had become a dictator during practice sessions, dismissing ideas and monopolizing strategies. Now, he wanted to make amends.

At the next practice, Arvind stood before the team, his heart pounding. "Before we start," he began, "I want to apologize. I haven't been a good leader. I've been controlling, dismissive, and unfair. I'm sorry."

The team members exchanged surprised glances but said nothing, waiting for him to continue.

"I want this to be a team effort," Arvind said. "From now on, I'll listen more. I'll respect your ideas. We're in this together."

One of the juniors, a girl named Priya, raised her hand hesitantly. "Does this mean we can suggest changes to the arguments?"

Arvind smiled. "Absolutely. Let's hear them."

For the first time in months, the room buzzed with genuine collaboration. The team's enthusiasm reignited something in Arvind—a reminder of why he had fallen in love with debate in the first place.

His final step was writing.

Late that evening, Arvind sat by the window in his dormitory, his notebook open on his lap. The moonlight spilled across the pages as he picked up his pen, his thoughts swirling.

He began to write—not for an assignment, not for a competition, but for himself. The words flowed, raw and unfiltered:

We falter, we fall, we lose our way,
Yet through the dark, we find our day.
In bonds once broken, hope takes flight,
A journey begins with a spark of light.

As the ink dried on the page, Arvind felt a weight lift from his chest. He wasn't fully healed, and the road ahead would be long, but for the first time in a long while, he felt ready to walk it.

The silence of the Hillspring Academy campus had always been a backdrop for Arvind's thoughts, but now, it had transformed into a mirror reflecting the depths of his soul. For weeks, he had been making amends, piecing together fragments of relationships he had shattered. Yet, as he walked the familiar paths of the school, he realized that healing his friendships was only one part of the journey. The harder task lay ahead: confronting himself.

The evening began in solitude.

Sitting by the fountain, Arvind opened his notebook, its pages bearing the weight of half-finished poems and unspoken fears. He tapped his pen against the paper, the rhythmic sound echoing in the stillness. The words Kabir had spoken under the peepal tree replayed in his mind: "You stopped listening to yourself."

For years, Arvind had prided himself on being self-aware, and on knowing his strengths and weaknesses. But now, he realized that his self-perception and introspection had been a carefully constructed facade—a mask of confidence hiding insecurities he hadn't dared to face.

What am I afraid of? he wrote at the top of the page. The question stared back at him, demanding an answer.

The first memories that surfaced were of his childhood.

Growing up, Arvind had always been the "smart one" in his family. His parents' praise had been a constant, their expectations an unspoken weight on his shoulders. Every report card, every certificate, every trophy had been met with proud smiles and words of affirmation.

But beneath their pride, Arvind had felt a quiet pressure—a need to excel, to prove that he was deserving of their admiration. He remembered nights spent at his desk, poring over textbooks until his eyes burned, not because he wanted to learn, but because he feared falling short.

When did success stop being about joy and start being about fear? he wrote.

The answer wasn't simple. It had been a gradual shift, a slow erosion of his passion as it became entangled with his need for validation. The debate had once been his escape, a space where he could express himself freely. But over time, it had morphed into a battlefield where every argument had to be a victory, every victory a testament to his worth.

Arvind's thoughts turned to his friendships.

Rahul's laughter, Kabir's calm advice, the late-night conversations that had once been the anchor of his days—he had taken them all for granted. And why? Because he had been so consumed by his ambitions he had failed to see the value of the people who stood by him.

When did I start seeing my friends as competitors instead of allies? he wrote.

The question hurt more than he expected. Rahul's success on the cricket field, and Kabir's quiet wisdom—they had never diminished his own achievements. Yet, his insecurities had twisted their strengths into threats, driving a wedge between them.

Arvind closed his eyes, the weight of his realizations pressing down on him. He had been running—not just from his friends, but from himself. He had been running from the fear of inadequacy, from the possibility that he might not be enough. And in doing so, he had lost sight of the person he wanted to be.

The breakthrough came with a single sentence.

It's okay to not be perfect.

The words felt foreign, almost rebellious, as he wrote them down. For so long, perfection had been his goal, his identity. But now, as he stared at the sentence, he felt a strange sense of relief. He didn't have to be perfect. He didn't have to have all the answers. He could make mistakes, stumble, and still find his way.

Arvind began to write again, the words flowing freely:

To chase the sun is not to own its light,
For shadows teach us truths of night.
To stumble, to fall, to rise anew,
Is life's true path, both old and true.

The poem felt like a release, a letting go of the weight he had been carrying. As he closed his notebook, Arvind felt a sense of clarity. The journey ahead wouldn't be easy, but for the first time, he wasn't afraid to face it.

CHAPTER NINE

A NEW APPROACH

The next morning, Arvind woke up feeling lighter. The heaviness of the past few months—the isolation, the self-doubt, the constant striving for perfection—seemed to have lifted, even if just slightly. He knew the road ahead would still be challenging, but for the first time, he felt equipped to walk it.

Arvind's first test came during debate practice.

The debate team had been preparing for an interschool competition, and tensions were high. As the team captain, Arvind had always taken it upon himself to craft the perfect strategy, often steamrolling over others' suggestions in the process. But today, he resolved to do things differently.

"Alright, let's hear your ideas," he said, addressing the group as they gathered in the library. His tone was measured, and open.

The team exchanged surprised glances before Priya, one of the junior members, hesitantly raised her hand. "I was thinking we could start with a personal anecdote to grab the audience's attention," she suggested. "It might make our argument more relatable."

Arvind nodded thoughtfully. "That's a great idea. Does anyone have a story in mind?"

Another team member chimed in, and soon the room was buzzing with collaborative energy. For the first time in months, the debate felt like a team effort rather than a one-man show. Arvind listened, contributed, and encouraged, realizing how much he had missed this sense of camaraderie.

By the end of the session, the team had crafted a compelling argument. As they packed up, Priya approached Arvind. "Thanks for letting us share our ideas," she said with a shy smile. "It felt... really good."

Arvind smiled back. "It's a team effort. You all have great ideas—I just needed to make room for them."

His next challenge was mending his relationship with his teachers.

Over the past months, Arvind's interactions with his teachers have become increasingly transactional. He had sought their approval, their validation, but had rarely engaged with them as mentors or guides. Now, he wanted to change that.

After class one afternoon, he approached Mrs. D'Souza, his English teacher, who had always encouraged his writing.

"Ma'am, do you have a moment?" he asked, hesitating at her desk.

She looked up, surprised but not unkind. "Of course, Arvind. What's on your mind?"

"I wanted to thank you," he began, "for always pushing me to write. I think I lost sight of how much it meant to me, but... I'm trying to find my way back to it."

Mrs. D'Souza's expression softened. "That's wonderful to hear, Arvind. Writing isn't just about the words—it's about understanding yourself. I'm glad you're rediscovering it."

They spoke for a while longer, and as Arvind left the classroom, he felt a renewed sense of purpose. Writing had always been his outlet, his way of making sense of the world. Now, it felt like a bridge—one that could reconnect him with himself and those around him.

The final test came in the form of Rahul.

While their earlier conversation had paved the way for rebonding, Arvind knew there was still work to be done. He found Rahul on the cricket field, as usual, practicing with his team.

"Rahul," Arvind called, walking onto the field. "Do you have a minute?"

Rahul glanced at him, his expression was neutral. "What's up?"

"I was wondering if we could grab a coffee or something after practice," Arvind said. "Just... catch up. Like old times."

Rahul hesitated, then nodded. "Sure. Give me twenty minutes."

They met at the campus café, a familiar spot where they had spent countless evenings joking and debating over cups of steaming chai. The conversation started awkwardly, filled with small talk about classes and campus events. But gradually, the tension eased, and they began to talk more openly.

"I missed this," Arvind admitted, stirring his tea. "I missed us."

Rahul leaned back in his chair, studying him. "You are trying, aren't you?"

"I am," Arvind said eagerly. "I know I have a long way to go, but... I don't want to lose what we had."

Rahul nodded slowly. "Alright. Let's see where this goes."

It wasn't a perfect resolution, but it was a step forward—one that filled Arvind with hope.

Arvind sat by the fountain that night, his notebook open on his lap. He writes:

To heal is not to erase the scar,
But to wear it proudly, for all we are.
Each step we take, though like a blunt knife,
Leads us closer to the heart of life.

As the words settle on the page, Arvind feels a quiet sense of accomplishment. He knows the journey isn't over, but he is finally moving in the right direction.

For the first time in months, Arvind felt a fragile but hopeful sense of balance returning to his life. His efforts to mend relationships with Rahul and Kabir had laid the foundation for healing, but he knew the journey was far from over. If he truly wanted to move forward, he had to confront not just his actions but the emotions that drove them.

These were the quiet moments of self-discovery that he needed. Arvind regularly sat alone at night with his diary open and wrote his heart out. In the beginning, he was reluctant to share the truth even with himself. But gradually he began discovering --- discovering Arvind Rathore.

One such similar night Arvind sat with his notebook, the blank pages illuminated by the soft glow of the campus lights. The gentle murmur of the fountain provided a soothing backdrop as he reflected on the moments that had shaped him—the triumphs, the failures, and everything in between. For years, he had been focused on the external markers of success: trophies, awards, and accolades. But now, he realized that those achievements had often been driven by a fear of inadequacy.

Why am I so afraid of failing? he wrote the question filling the page with quiet urgency.

The answer wasn't immediate, but as he sat there, memories began to flash. He thought of his childhood, of the pride in his parents' eyes whenever he excelled. Their praise had always been genuine, but somewhere along the way, he had internalized the belief that his worth was tied to his accomplishments. The thought both saddened and freed him. Maybe it's okay to fail, he thought. Maybe failure is part of growing.

The next day brought an unexpected opportunity for vulnerability.

During a group discussion in English class, Mrs. D'Souza asked the students to share a personal story that had shaped their perspective on life. Most of the class was hesitant at the prospect of opening up, but Arvind found himself raising his hand.

"When I was younger," he began, his voice steady but soft, "I thought success was the only thing that mattered. I pushed myself to be the best at everything, and for a while, it worked. But along the way, I started losing the things that mattered—my friends, my joy, even my sense of self."

The room grew quiet as his classmates listened intently. Arvind hesitated, then continued. "It's been hard, trying to fix things. But I've realized that being vulnerable, and admitting when I'm wrong, is a kind of strength too. And it's helped me reconnect with the people I care about."

When he finished, there was a pause before Mrs. D'Souza spoke. "Thank you, Arvind. That was brave."

The class erupted into applause, but what mattered most to Arvind was the look of understanding on Rahul's face and the slight nod from Kabir.

Later that week, Arvind faced a new challenge in the form of a junior debate team practice.

As part of his efforts to give back to the community, he volunteered to mentor the younger students. Standing before the group of eager faces, he felt a mix of excitement and nerves. Would they listen to him? Would they see through his efforts?

"Alright," he began, "before we dive into strategies, I want to know what debate means to you. Why do you do it?"

One by one, the juniors shared their reasons. Some loved the thrill of argument, others enjoyed the camaraderie of team practices, and a few simply wanted to improve their public speaking skills. As Arvind listened, he realized how much he had missed this raw enthusiasm.

"Those are all great reasons," he said, smiling. "But remember, debate isn't just about winning. It's about understanding different perspectives, about growing as a thinker and a communicator. And most importantly, it's about enjoying the journey."

By the end of the session, the juniors were buzzing with ideas, and Arvind felt a renewed sense of purpose. Guiding them reminded him of why he had fallen in love with debate in the first place.

To stand exposed, with fears in view,
Is the bravest thing a heart can do.
For strength lies not in masks we wear,
But in the truths we choose to share.

As the words settled on the page, Arvind felt a quiet sense of fulfillment. He still had a long way to go, but he was beginning to understand that true strength came from embracing vulnerability and staying true to himself.

CHAPTER TEN

EMBRACING THE PRESENT

The rhythm of life at Hillspring Academy began to change for Arvind. For months, he had operated in a state of restless ambition, chasing achievements without truly enjoying the journey. But now, with each passing day, he found himself more grounded in the present moment, appreciating the simple joys that had once gone unnoticed.

The first sign of change came during an impromptu cricket match.

One afternoon, as Arvind walked past the field, he spotted Rahul waving him over. "We're short a player," Rahul called. "Want to join?"

Arvind hesitated. He had always walked away from sports, convinced that his lack of skill would make him an easy target for ridicule. But something about Rahul's easy smile made him pause. "Alright," he said, stepping onto the field.

The game was chaotic and unstructured, filled with laughter and good-natured teasing. Arvind's batting was clumsy, and his fielding left much to be desired, but for the first time, he didn't mind. When he finally managed to hit a ball past the boundary, the team erupted in cheers, and Arvind couldn't help but laugh along with them.

As the game ended and the players dispersed, Rahul clapped him on the back. "Not bad for a bookworm," he teased.

Arvind grinned. "Don't get used to it. I'm still more comfortable with a pen than a bat."

"Maybe," Rahul said, his tone softer now. "But it's good to see you out here. We've missed you."

The words stayed with Arvind long after the game ended. They were a reminder that connection didn't have to be perfect to be meaningful.

A quiet conversation with Kabir brought another layer of clarity.

A few days later, Arvind found Kabir sitting under the peepal tree, his notebook open on his lap. The sight was familiar and comforting. Without hesitation, Arvind joined him.

"Writing something new?" Arvind asked, gesturing to the notebook.

Kabir nodded. "Just jotting down thoughts. Nothing fancy."

For a while, they sat in comfortable silence, the rustling leaves providing a soothing backdrop. Then, Kabir spoke. "You've changed, you know."

Arvind looked at him, surprised. "In a good way, I hope."

Kabir smiled. "In the best way. You're... present now. You listen. You care. It's good to see."

Arvind felt a swell of gratitude. "You were right, Kabir. About everything. And I'm sorry it took me so long to realize it."

Kabir shook his head. "Growth takes time, Arvind. The important thing is that you're trying."

The conversation left Arvind feeling lighter, and more assured in his path forward.

That night, as he sat by his desk, and began to write:

The present is a gift we often ignore,
Chasing futures or reliving before.
But here, in this moment, life softly speaks,
In laughter, in silence, in the bonds we seek.

He wasn't chasing perfection anymore. He was learning to live, to be, and to appreciate the beauty of the present.

CHAPTER ELEVEN

Too much in the other Direction?

The golden hues of sunset bathed the Hillspring Academy campus as Arvind walked toward the debate hall. His mind buzzed with anticipation; he had been preparing a group of juniors for the upcoming interschool debate competition, and their progress had been impressive. For the first time in months, he felt a deep purpose—not to win, but to guide and inspire.

The evening began with a heated discussion during practice.

The juniors debated a contentious topic: "Whether technological advancements had done more harm than good." Their enthusiasm turned into interruptions as the discussion unfolded, and voices began to clash. Arvind watched from the sidelines, unsure of how to intervene without dampening their spirit.

"Enough," a junior named Neha snapped, glaring at her teammate. "If you're not going to stick to the framework, why are you even here?"

The room fell silent, and the tension increased. Arvind stepped forward, his voice calm but firm. "Neha, that's not how we address each other."

Neha crossed her arms, and her frustration was evident. "But she's not taking this seriously! How are we supposed to win if half the team doesn't care?"

Arvind took a deep breath, choosing his words carefully. "Winning isn't the only goal here. This is about learning, about growing together as a team. If we can't respect each other, what's the point?"

Neha looked away, her cheeks flushing. The teammate in question fidgeted nervously but gave Arvind a grateful nod. The group resumed their discussion, this time with more patience. Yet, as the session progressed, Arvind couldn't shake the feeling that something deeper was brewing beneath the surface.

The conflict came to a head later that evening.

As Arvind walked back to his dormitory, he overheard a conversation near the fountain. Neha and a few other juniors were sitting in a circle, their voices low but strained.

"I don't get why Arvind's so soft now," Neha said, her tone tinged with bitterness. "He used to be so focused, so driven. Now it's all about feelings and teamwork. It's like he doesn't care if we win."

Another student chimed in. "Yeah, but isn't this better? He listens to us now."

"Sure, but where's the edge? Where's the Arvind who pushed everyone to be their best?"

Arvind felt a knot form in his stomach. He stepped back, unsure whether to confront them or walk away. The old Arvind would have marched over, demanding an explanation. But now, he hesitated, the weight of his new perspective holding him back.

The introspection that followed was deeply unsettling.

Back in his room, Arvind sat by the window, his notebook open but untouched. Neha's words echoed in his mind: "Where's the Arvind who pushed everyone to be their best?" Had he swung too far in the other direction? In trying to be kind and inclusive, had he lost the drive that once defined him?

He wrote tentatively:

To push too hard is to risk breaking,
To try too soft is to risk forsaking.
Where lies the balance, the path so thin,
Between striving to win and letting others in?

The lines brought little clarity. Arvind stared at them, frustration bubbling beneath his calm appearance. Change wasn't supposed to feel this uncertain, this fragile. Had he made the right choices? Or had he compromised too much of himself?

A conversation with Kabir provided perspective.

The next morning, Arvind sought out Kabir by the peepal tree. Kabir was reading, but he set the book aside when he saw Arvind's troubled expression.

"What's on your mind?" Kabir asked, his tone steady.

Arvind hesitated before speaking. "Do you think I've changed too much? That I've lost... what made me, me?"

Kabir studied him for a moment before replying. "Change doesn't mean losing yourself, Arvind. It means finding a better version of yourself. Why do you ask?"

Arvind recounted Neha's words, his doubts spilling out in a rush. When he finished, Kabir nodded thoughtfully.

"You're trying to find balance," Kabir said. "And that's hard. But remember, being a leader isn't about pleasing everyone. It's about knowing when to listen and when to stand firm."

"But what if I'm wrong?" Arvind asked.

"Then you learn," Kabir said simply. "That's part of the process."

Arvind's resolve was tested during the next practice.

When he entered the debate hall, the juniors were already gathered, their tension evident. Neha glanced at him but quickly looked away. Arvind took a deep breath before addressing the group.

"I heard some of your concerns," he began, his voice steady. "And I understand where you're coming from. You want to win, and you feel like I'm not pushing you hard enough. That's fair."

The group exchanged uncertain glances. Arvind continued. "But I want you to understand something. Winning isn't just about out-arguing the other team. It's about being prepared, being confident, and working together. If we can't trust each other, we've already lost."

Neha spoke up, her tone softer this time. "We just... don't want to let you down."

Arvind smiled. "You won't. As long as you give it your best, I'll be proud of you. Now, let's focus on what we can improve."

The session that followed was one of their best yet. The juniors worked with renewed energy, and for the first time, Arvind felt like he had struck the right balance—encouraging without compromising, leading without dictating.

To lead is to listen, to guide with care,
To shoulder the weight that others can't bear.
In balance, we find the strength to grow,
A journey of learning, as rivers flow.

He wasn't perfect, but he was learning—and that, he realized, was enough.

CHAPTER TWELVE

THE DEBATE

The day of the interschool debate competition dawned bright and clear, the crisp morning air buzzing with anticipation. Hillspring Academy's auditorium was alive with activity as teams from across the region arrived, their nervous chatter filling the space. For Arvind, the event wasn't just a competition—it was a culmination of everything he had been working toward, both as a mentor and as a person.

The atmosphere was electric as the team gathered backstage.

Arvind stood with the juniors, their energy a mix of excitement and nerves. Priya, who had struggled the most in practice, clutched her cue cards tightly, her knuckles were white. Neha paced the floor, her expression tense but focused.

"Take a deep breath," Arvind said, addressing the group. "You've got this. Remember, it's not just about winning—it's about showing who we are and what we stand for. Trust yourselves and each other."

Neha stopped pacing and looked at him. "We won't let you down."

Arvind smiled. "You've already made me proud. Now go show everyone else what you can do."

The first round began with Hillspring Academy up against their toughest rival.

The topic—"Whether artificial intelligence posed a greater benefit or threat to society"—was one Arvind had helped the team prepare extensively for. Neha opened the argument with a commanding presence, her points sharp and well-articulated. Priya followed, her delivery steady despite the slight tremor in her voice. The team's final speaker, a boy named Rohan, closed with a passionate rebuttal that earned enthusiastic applause from the audience.

As the judges deliberated, Arvind watched his team with a mix of pride and nervousness. When the results were announced, Hillspring Academy advanced to the next round, their victory met with cheers and high-fives.

The second round brought unexpected challenges.

The topic was announced moments before the debate: "Should traditional education systems be replaced by online learning?" The team had limited time to prepare, and tensions rose as they scrambled to organize their arguments.

"This is a curveball," Neha muttered, her eyebrow creased as she scribbled notes. "We didn't prepare for this."

"Focus on what we know," Arvind said, his voice calm. "Play to our strengths—use examples, statistics, personal anecdotes. We can do this."

Despite the pressure, the team rallied, delivering a performance that was far from perfect but brimming with sincerity and resilience. When the round ended, Arvind saw the relief on their faces and felt a surge of admiration for their determination.

The final round was the ultimate test.

Hillspring Academy faced off against Megha Reddy's team, the reigning champions. The topic—"Is competition necessary for personal growth?"—was one that struck a personal chord with Arvind. As the juniors prepared their arguments, he couldn't help but reflect on his own journey.

When the debate began, the tension in the room was rocketing. Megha's team opened with polished, confident arguments, their delivery seamless. But Hillspring Academy's team responded with a raw authenticity that captured the audience's attention. Neha's rebuttal was particularly powerful, blending logic with emotion as she spoke about the importance of balancing competition with compassion.

As the final speaker, Priya stepped forward, her voice steady and clear. "Competition pushes us to grow," she concluded, "but growth is meaningless if we lose sight of our humanity. True success lies not in defeating others, but in lifting each other."

The room erupted in applause, and Arvind felt a lump form in his throat. Priya's words encapsulated everything he had been striving to teach—not just to his team, but to himself.

The results were announced to a hushed audience.

Hillspring Academy placed second, narrowly losing to Megha's team. There was a brief moment of disappointment, but it was quickly overshadowed by the team's sense of accomplishment. They had given their best, and it showed.

As the audience dispersed, Megha approached Arvind, her expression unreadable. "Your team surprised me," she admitted. "They've got heart. That's rare."

"Thanks," Arvind said, his voice genuine. "Your team was incredible, as always."

Megha smiled faintly. "Don't go soft on them, though. They've got potential."

Arvind nodded, her words a reminder of the balance he was still learning to navigate.

That evening, Arvind sat by the fountain, his notebook open on his lap. The moonlight reflected off the water as he wrote:

In striving, we grow, in falling, we learn,
The fire within is what we must earn.
But hearts united, in loss or in gain,
Show us the strength that will always remain.

CHAPTER THIRTEEN

The Echoes of Efforts

The day after the debate competition, Hillspring Academy buzzed with a renewed sense of pride. The juniors who had represented the school returned to their usual routines, but their conversations were laced with reflections on the experience. For Arvind, the event marked a significant milestone—not because of the results, but because of the journey it represented.

The morning began with a surprise assembly.

The school principal, Mr. Iyer, addressed the students with his characteristic gravitas. "Yesterday, our debate team demonstrated not just skill but heart. Though they may not have taken first place, they achieved something far more important—they reminded us of the values we hold dear: integrity, perseverance, and collaboration."

He gestured for the team to stand, and the auditorium erupted into applause. Arvind felt a mix of pride and humility as he stood with the juniors, their faces beaming with a shared sense of accomplishment.

Later that day, Priya approached Arvind in the library, her expression thoughtful. "I wanted to thank you," she said, her voice quiet. "For believing in us, even when we didn't believe in ourselves."

Arvind smiled. "You didn't need me to believe in you. You've always had what it takes—I just helped you see it."

Priya hesitated, then added, "I was so scared during the final round. But when I looked at you, I realized I didn't have to be perfect. I just had to try."

Her words struck a chord with Arvind, echoing his own journey of letting go of perfection. "That's all any of us can do," he said. "And you did more than try—you shone."

Rahul and Kabir offered their own perspectives during a late-night chat too.

That evening, the trio gathered by the fountain, a place that had come to symbolize their shared growth. Rahul leaned back, his gaze on the stars. "You know, watching you with those juniors reminded me of when we first started debating. You've come a long way, Arvind."

Kabir nodded, his tone reflective. "You've found a balance—not just in how you lead, but in how you live. That's not easy."

Arvind chuckled softly. "It's still a work in progress."

"And that's okay," Kabir said. "The important thing is that you're trying—and that you're listening."

Their conversation drifted into laughter and memories of their earlier years.

The chapter concludes with Arvind writing in his notebook.

Back in his dorm room, Arvind opened his notebook and began to write:

The echoes of effort, in loss or success,
Remind us of growth, the weight we confess.
For journeys are measured in steps, not in gold,
In the truths we embrace, the stories retold.

As the ink dried on the page, Arvind felt a quiet sense of fulfillment. The competition was over, but the lessons it imparted would stay with him for years to come. For the first time, he felt ready to embrace whatever challenges lay ahead—not as an ever-longing achiever, but as a leader who understood the power of connection.

The aftermath of the debate competition brought calm to Hillspring Academy, but for Arvind, it also marked the start of a new chapter in his life. The lessons learned from the competition continued to resonate, shaping his interactions and decisions. Yet, with every step forward, there was a sense of anticipation—a feeling that the real challenges lay ahead.

A conversation with Kabir set the tone for this new phase.

One afternoon, as they walked through the campus gardens, Kabir turned to Arvind. "You've been quieter lately," he observed. "Thinking about something?"

Arvind nodded. "I guess I'm wondering... what's next? The competition felt like such a turning point, but now that it's over, I feel this... weight. Like I'm supposed to do something bigger."

Kabir smiled faintly. "Growth doesn't always come with a clear roadmap. Sometimes, it's about taking the next step, even if you're not sure where it leads."

The simplicity of Kabir's advice struck a chord. Arvind realized that he had been so focused on monumental goals that he had overlooked the value of small, meaningful actions.

The weight of leadership manifested in unexpected ways.

With the debate team's success, Arvind found himself in the spotlight more than ever. Juniors sought his guidance, teachers praised his growth, and even his peers began to view him with a newfound respect. But with recognition came expectations, and Arvind felt the pressure to live up to the image others had of him.

One evening, a junior named Varun approached him in the library. "Arvind, can I ask you something?" he began hesitantly.

"Of course," Arvind replied, setting aside his book.

Varun fidgeted with his notebook. "How do you stay so confident? I mean, even when things get tough?"

Arvind considered the question carefully. "I don't think it's about always feeling confident," he said slowly. "It's about accepting that it's okay to be uncertain sometimes. Confidence comes from knowing you'll figure it out, even if you don't have all the answers right away."

Varun nodded, a thoughtful look on his face. "Thanks, Arvind. That... helps."

As Varun walked away, Arvind realized that his own words were as much a reminder to himself as they were advice to others.

A moment of vulnerability tested his resolve.

A few days later, Arvind received an email from the organizers of a national-level debate competition. They were inviting him to represent Hillspring Academy as an individual participant—a rare honor. But the invitation came with a caveat: he would need to prepare a solo argument on a topic he hadn't encountered before, and the competition was only two weeks away.

The prospect was both thrilling and daunting. Arvind had spent months focusing on teamwork and collaboration, and the idea of returning to the solitary pursuit of excellence stirred old insecurities. Could he balance his newfound approach with the demands of individual competition?

He sought advice from Rahul and Kabir that evening. Sitting by the fountain, he shared the news and his concerns.

"What do you think I should do?" he asked, his voice tinged with uncertainty.

Rahul grinned. "I think you already know the answer, Arvind. You've just got to trust yourself."

Kabir nodded in agreement. "This isn't about proving anything to anyone. It's about challenging yourself—and you've always been good at that."

Their encouragement gave Arvind the clarity he needed. He decided to accept the invitation, viewing it not as a test of his abilities, but as an opportunity to grow.

CHAPTER FOURTEEN

BECOMING WHOLE

The evening before the national-level debate competition, Hillspring Academy was unusually quiet. Most of the students had retired early, the weight of the approaching midterms dulling the usual energy of the dormitories. Arvind, however, was wide awake, seated at his desk with a notebook open before him. The title of his speech—"The Ethics of Artificial Intelligence in Modern Society"—was scrawled across the top of the page in bold, decisive letters.

But tonight, the argument wasn't his focus. The thoughts swirling in his mind had little to do with the competition itself and everything to do with the journey that had led him here.

A quiet moment of introspection began as he stared at his reflection in the window.

For months, Arvind had been reshaping his identity, peeling back the layers of ego and self-doubt to find something truer beneath. Now, as he prepared for one of the most important events of his academic life, he couldn't help but question: What does it all mean?

He picked up his pen and began to write, his thoughts spilling onto the page:

To lead is to listen, to speak is to hear,
The self we discover through doubt and through fear.
For growth is not linear, nor is it swift,
It's the pain and the joy that together uplift.

The words flowed easily, but they carried the weight of months of reflection. Arvind set the pen down and closed his eyes, letting his mind drift.

His inner dialogue took him back to pivotal moments.

In the stillness of the night, Arvind revisited the conversations that had shaped his journey. Kabir's steady wisdom, Rahul's unwavering support, even Neha's critiques—all of them had played a role in his transformation.

"You've stopped listening to yourself," Kabir had said under the peepal tree, his tone gentle but firm. That single sentence had unraveled Arvind's carefully constructed facade, forcing him to confront the insecurities he had buried deep within. He smiled faintly at the memory, grateful for Kabir's honesty.

Rahul's words echoed next: "You've got to trust yourself." Trust had always been the hardest part—trusting that his worth wasn't tied to perfection, that his friendships could survive his flaws, that he could find balance in the chaos.

And then there were the juniors. Priya's hesitant gratitude, Neha's fiery determination, the team's collective triumphs and struggles—they had taught him that leadership wasn't about control but about connection. He had learned as much from them as they had from him, if not more.

The weight of gratitude brought clarity.

Arvind opened his eyes and gazed at the notebook in front of him. For the first time, he felt a profound sense of wholeness—not because he had all the answers, but because he had learned to embrace the uncertainty.

He wrote:

To be whole is not to be perfect, but to be real,
To embrace every scar, every wound we conceal.
For in our imperfection, we find our truth,
A lesson that echoes from age to youth.

The morning of the competition arrived.

The auditorium buzzed with energy as participants and spectators filled the space. Arvind stood backstage, his speech memorized but his heart unusually calm. As he adjusted the microphone on his lapel, he caught his reflection in a nearby mirror. This time, the face staring back at him didn't feel like a stranger.

When his name was called, Arvind stepped onto the stage, his steps steady and purposeful. The spotlight was bright, the audience a blur of faces, but he focused on the podium before him. Taking a deep breath, he began:

"Good morning. Today, we stand at the intersection of progress and ethics, a crossroads that demands not just answers, but understanding..."

As the words flowed, Arvind felt a quiet confidence settle over him. This wasn't about proving himself. It wasn't about winning. It was about sharing a perspective, connecting with others, and staying true to the values he had worked so hard to rediscover.

That evening, Arvind sat by the fountain, the familiar sound of trickling water grounding him. The competition results had been announced—he had placed second, a result that might have once crushed him. But now, it felt like an affirmation of his journey. He had given his best, and that was enough.

Opening his notebook, he wrote:

To chase the sun is to feel its glow,
To stand in its warmth, to let it show.
For journeys end, but they also begin,
A cycle of growth, a victory within.

As the ink dried, Arvind closed the notebook and leaned back, gazing at the stars. He didn't know what challenges lay ahead, but for the first time, he wasn't afraid. He had found his balance, his purpose, and most importantly, himself.